This book belongs to

o o o o o o o o o o o o o o o

For Phil, Sean, Bethany, and Joey – my inspiration. Love you all x – S.W.

For Dylan – T.W.

What small

OXFORD
UNIVERSITY PRESS

Great Clarendon Street, Oxford OX2 6DP

Oxford University Press is a department of the University of Oxford.
It furthers the University's objective of excellence in research, scholarship,
and education by publishing worldwide in

Oxford New York

Auckland Cape Town Dar es Salaam Hong Kong Karachi
Kuala Lumpur Madrid Melbourne Mexico City Nairobi
New Delhi Shanghai Taipei Toronto

With offices in
Argentina Austria Brazil Chile Czech Republic France Greece
Guatemala Hungary Italy Japan Poland Portugal Singapore
South Korea Switzerland Thailand Turkey Ukraine Vietnam

Text copyright © Sheryl Webster 2010
Illustrations copyright © Tim Warnes 2010
The moral rights of the author and artist have been asserted

Database right Oxford University Press (maker)

First published 2010

British Library Cataloguing in Publication Data available

ISBN: 978-0-19-272868-5 (paperback)

10 9 8 7 6 5 4 3 2 1

Printed in China

Paper used in the production of this book is a natural, recyclable product made
from wood grown in sustainable forests. The manufacturing process conforms
to the environmental regulations of the country of origin

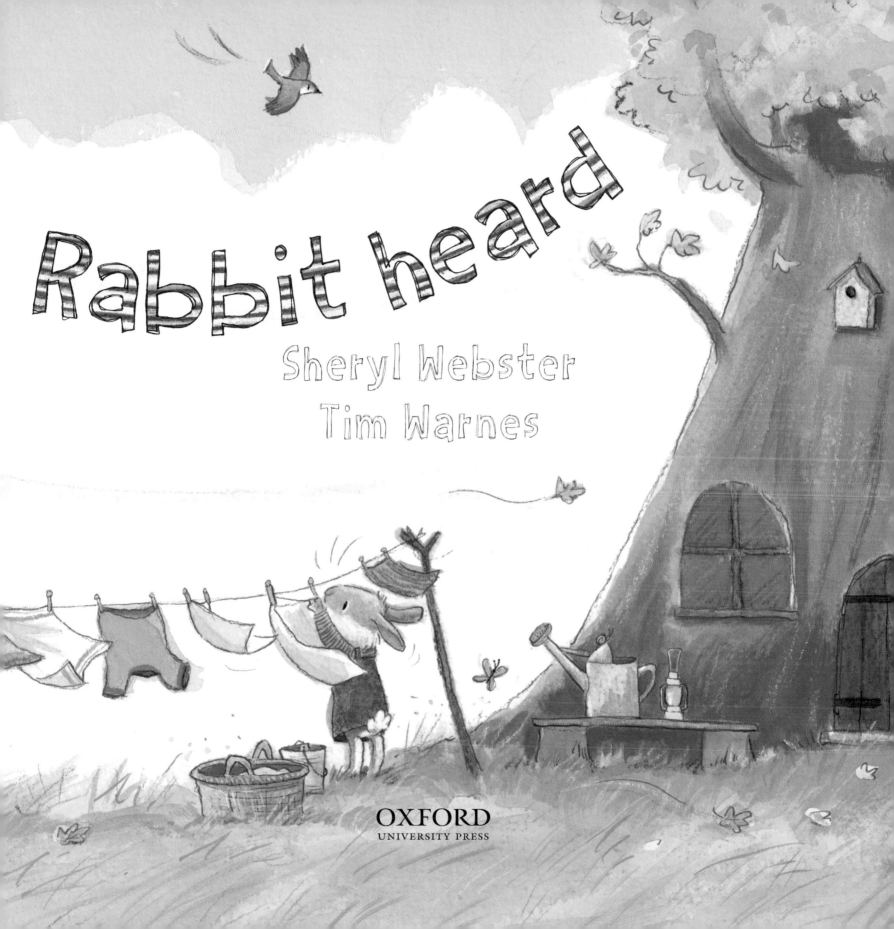

Rabbit heard

Sheryl Webster

Tim Warnes

OXFORD
UNIVERSITY PRESS

Small Rabbit did not
want to go for a walk.

'It's too cold! I'm too busy . . . and I'm too tired!'

'It's not cold, it's fresh,' said Big Rabbit.
'You're not busy, you're playing.
And you are certainly not yet tired!'

'Well, it's too windy. It won't be fun.'

'Of course it will be fun,' said Big Rabbit. 'Now off we go.'

Outside the wind howled.
Whooooo!

Small Rabbit
began to
hop and skip
to keep
himself warm.

Big Rabbit wanted Small Rabbit
to stay close.

'Try to keep up,' she said.
But Big Rabbit's words were
lost in the howl of the wind.

What Small Rabbit
heard was . . .

'Jump in the mud.'

So he did.

The wind howled. **Whooooo!**
It picked up a pile of leaves
and they danced past Small Rabbit.

He began to chase them.
Big Rabbit shivered
and shouted,
'Stay with me, please.'

Again her words were
lost in the howl of the wind.

What Small Rabbit
heard was . . .

'Roll in the leaves.'
So he did!

Soon they came to Thistledown Field.

'Yippee!' yelled Small Rabbit, pointing to the animals.
Big Rabbit called to Small Rabbit
as she tried to catch up,

'I want you to wait!'

The wind howled. **Whooooo!**

PLEASE SHUT
THE GATE

What Small Rabbit heard was . . .

'Open the gate.'
So he did!

Small Rabbit raced up the hill.
It was getting colder and his
coat flapped in the wind as he ran.

Big Rabbit was still trying to close the gate but she cried out, 'Fasten your coat.'

The wind howled.

Whooooo!

What Small Rabbit heard was . . .

'Ride on the goat.'
So he did . . .

all the way to the top of the hill!

Big Rabbit was worried that Small Rabbit
might get blown off the top, and she
shouted as loudly as she could,

'Keep very still.'

But it was her words that were blown away.
What Small Rabbit heard was . . .

'Roll down
the hill.'
So he did.

Big Rabbit was quite out of
puff and she could think of only
one way to catch up.

She shouted as she rolled,

'Wait for meeeee!'

The wind howled
all around.

What Small Rabbit
heard was . . .

'Climb the treeeee.'
So he did.

Small Rabbit swung from a branch. Suddenly, he spotted his rabbit hole on the other side of the stream and he started to hop home.

A thought flashed through Big Rabbit's mind.
She looked at how dirty Small Rabbit was.
She thought of their lovely clean burrow.

'Small Rabbit, don't go inside!' she pleaded.

The wind howled.

Whooooo!

Big Rabbit peeked cautiously into the burrow.
She tiptoed in.

It was quiet. Too quiet.
Very slowly, she opened the cupboard door.

'Boo!'
laughed Small Rabbit.
'It took me ages to find somewhere to hide.

But I did!'

Small Rabbit leapt into Big Rabbit's arms.
'Windy walks are lots and lots of fun!' he said.

And Big Rabbit had to agree.

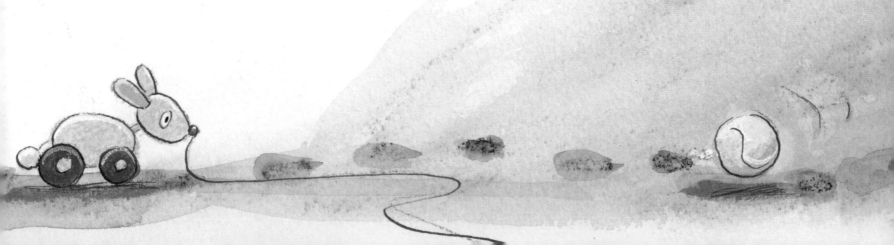